Beauty
and the
Beast

URSULA JONES SARAH GIBB

ORCHARD

Beauty
and the
Beast

For my 'little ghosts', Abigail, Claudia and Felicity.
U.J.

For Harrison and Isabella, with love.
S.G.

ORCHARD BOOKS
338 Euston Road, London NW1 3BH
Orchard Books Australia
Level 17/207 Kent Street, Sydney, NSW 2000

First published in 2012 by Orchard Books
First published in paperback in 2013

ISBN 978 1 40831 272 8

Text © Ursula Jones 2012
Illustrations © Sarah Gibb 2012

A CIP catalogue record for this book is
available from the British Library.

1 3 5 7 9 10 8 6 4 2

Printed in China

Orchard Books is a division of Hachette Children's Books,
an Hachette UK company.

www.hachette.co.uk

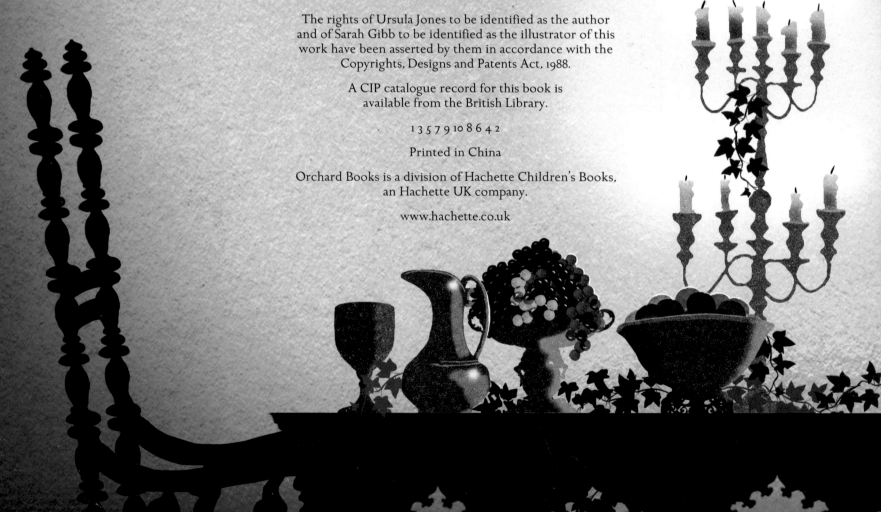

Once there was a rich merchant who had three daughters. The two eldest were very pretty, but the youngest daughter was beautiful, so everyone called her Beauty. That made her sisters horribly jealous.

All the young men in the city wanted to marry Beauty's sisters, but they were picky about husbands. One sister was waiting for a duke and the other wouldn't leave the house for less than a prince. Several suitors asked Beauty to marry them, but she preferred to stay at home with her father, reading her books and playing the piano.

Then came a bad day. The merchant lost his fortune.

"Does that mean we're poor now?" Beauty asked her father. And all the suitors backed out of the room so fast they jammed in the doorway.

"Was it something I said?" Beauty asked.

"Stupid!" her sisters snapped at her. "They don't want to marry a *poor* bride. None of us will get a husband now." And Beauty was sorry to hear that.

Their father explained that their house was sold, but he still had a little place in the country where they could live. And away they drove, out of the city.

They travelled for miles and miles. The two older sisters were horrified by the countryside. It was full of plants! And not a clothes shop in sight! Eventually, their father pulled up in front of a ramshackle little building.

"Why have we stopped at this ruin?" they asked.

"This is it," he said. "This is our new home." And the two sisters had hysterics.

"We'll soon learn to look after ourselves and be farmers," their father comforted them.

But he was wrong. It took Beauty and her father two whole years to learn how to farm. The sisters wouldn't even try. They stayed in bed till ten every morning, then put on their best rags and trudged off for their daily walk.

"You never know," they would say. "We may find a suitor hidden behind one of these ghastly trees." But they never did.

Then came good news. A ship the merchant thought was lost at sea had come into harbour. He set out for the city at once.

"We shall be rich again," the sisters said gleefully, and they gave him a list of presents to bring back: fur coats, diamond tiaras and dresses galore.

"And what shall I buy for you, Beauty?" her father asked, mounting his horse. Beauty felt sorry for the horse – he'd hardly be able to carry a thing more once he was loaded down with her sisters' orders. "Bring me a rose, Father," she said, and she waved him goodbye.

Then came bad news. All the money from the ship's cargo was used to pay off the merchant's debts, and he rode home poorer than ever. It began to snow, so he took a shortcut through the forest. But an icy wind blew the snow into a violent blizzard and he lost his way. He knew he would soon die of cold, and then what would become of his daughters?

Suddenly, he saw a light through the trees. He staggered towards it and found an avenue that led him to a deserted courtyard. His horse trotted into a stable and set to work on some hay.

A blast of wind swept the falling snow aside and the merchant saw a vast mansion ahead with candlelight twinkling in each window. He stumbled through the snow to the front door and knocked. It swung open, and he entered a dining hall with a log fire and a table laid out with supper for one person.

Steam rose from his soaked coat as he warmed himself at the fire and waited for the owner of the house to arrive. But no one came. He was starving. By eleven o'clock he gave in and ate the supper himself. Then he found a bedroom and fell fast asleep.

The next morning, the merchant looked down from his bedroom window onto a garden of flowers. The deep snow had disappeared. "This place is a bit strange," he murmured. "Time to leave." But his clothes were missing, which was awkward. He had no choice but to put on a new suit that was laid out on a chair. It fitted perfectly. Downstairs, there was a cup of hot chocolate on the table – his favourite breakfast! – so he drank it.

"My thanks to the good fairy that owns this house," he called, and he set off through the gardens to find his horse. As he passed under an archway of roses, he remembered Beauty's request and picked one for her.

At once an ear-crunching noise blared. It frightened the wits out of him. And there, barring his way, was the most terrifying, foulest creature he had ever seen. Even more terrifying – it could talk!

"Ungrateful man!" it growled. "After all I've given you, you steal my roses. Die!"

The merchant fell over in terror, pleading for his life. "I meant no harm, my lord," he gabbled.

"The name's Beast," it snarled.

"I picked it for my daughter, Beast, sir. Please don't kill me."

"All right. I won't," growled the Beast. "I'll kill your daughter instead. Bring her to me. Get on your horse and fetch her. There's a chest of gold to go with you. Bring your daughter here in three months or die yourself."

The merchant promised to do as the Beast asked, though really he had no intention of letting Beauty die such a terrible death. He meant to go and say goodbye to his girls, give them the gold, then come back himself to die.

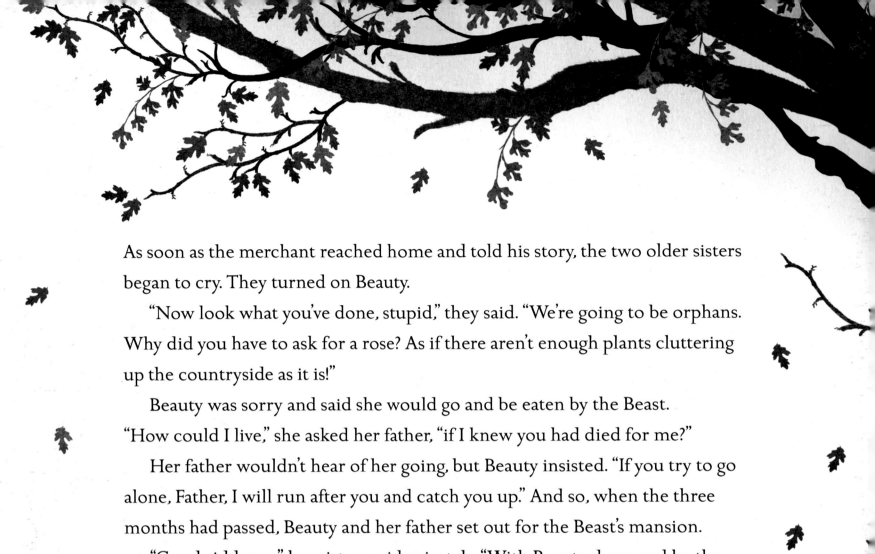

As soon as the merchant reached home and told his story, the two older sisters began to cry. They turned on Beauty.

"Now look what you've done, stupid," they said. "We're going to be orphans. Why did you have to ask for a rose? As if there aren't enough plants cluttering up the countryside as it is!"

Beauty was sorry and said she would go and be eaten by the Beast. "How could I live," she asked her father, "if I knew you had died for me?"

Her father wouldn't hear of her going, but Beauty insisted. "If you try to go alone, Father, I will run after you and catch you up." And so, when the three months had passed, Beauty and her father set out for the Beast's mansion.

"Good riddance," her sisters said privately. "With Beauty devoured by the Beast, there will be more of that chest of gold for us. And gold brings in suitors. And suitors mean wedding bells." But they rubbed their eyes with onion to make it look as if they were crying bitterly to see Beauty ride to her death.

The Beast's mansion was the same as before – the stable for the horse, the fire burning in the hall – but this time, the supper on the table was for two. But they couldn't eat. The merchant was too unhappy and Beauty was too scared. The clock struck nine. Instantly the awful, ear-crunching noise blared.

"He's coming," whispered Beauty's father. "Farewell, daughter."

Then the Beast appeared. He was more terrifying than Beauty had ever imagined. He gave a disgusting snort when he saw her and growled, "Has she come of her own accord?"

But Beauty replied, "Yes, I have," so calmly, no one would have guessed how frightened she was.

"Thank you," said the Beast. "Now eat up and go to bed. And you," he growled at her father, "you clear off first thing in the morning – for good."

The next morning, Beauty said goodbye to her father and he rode away sobbing. Beauty sat and cried too and waited to die. But the Beast didn't come and devour her, so she stopped crying and decided to fill in the time till he did by exploring his mansion. It was a beautiful but lonely place. Still the Beast didn't come. She found a door labelled 'Beauty's Room' and in she went.

The room was filled with books. There was a piano too, and a golden bowl of chocolates that never emptied, no matter how many she ate. There were paints and paper and pencils and rulers and a chemistry set. Whoever had got the room ready didn't mean Beauty to be bored.

She opened a book and read, 'Your wish is our command. You are queen and mistress here'.

"Then I wish I could see my father," Beauty sighed.

At once, the words 'the mirror, the mirror' formed on the page. Beauty looked into the mirror on the wall and saw her father arriving home. He was in tears. Her sisters were not.

That evening, Beauty was about to start her supper when the clock struck nine and she heard the ear-crunching noise. The Beast was coming. 'This is it,' she thought. 'Now I shall be *his* supper.'

The Beast appeared. Beauty waited to die, but all he said was, "May I watch you dine?"

"You're the master."

"No, you're the mistress, Beauty. I'll go if you want."

"I'd like you to stay," she said politely, crossing her fingers behind her back.

Then he asked, "Do you think I'm ugly?"

"Yes, I do. Very." She didn't want to make him angry so she added truthfully, "But I think you're good."

The Beast said, "I'm stupid, though."

"I am too," said Beauty. "My sisters are always telling me I am. That makes two of us. So cheer up."

"All right," said the Beast. "I'm still a monster, though."

"There are monsters and monsters," said Beauty.

"What does that mean?"

"It means that some monsters look awful, but inside they are really very kind, and some people look very kind, but inside they are really monsters."

"I'm a bit too stupid to follow that."

"I'm not sure I follow it myself now," laughed Beauty. The Beast made a noise she hoped was a laugh too; a glugging sound like water running down a plughole. After the last glug he said, "Beauty, will you be my wife?"

Beauty nearly choked on a roast potato with shock. She was terrified of enraging him but she said, "No, Beast. I won't." The Beast sighed a whistling, sad sigh, and vanished.

This went on for three months. Beauty got used to her peculiar life. There was always so much to do, and each day there was a new and ever more stunning dress to wear.

She began to look forward to the Beast's visits at nine o'clock, but he always spoiled their talk with the same question: "Beauty, will you be my wife?"

"I'll always be your friend," Beauty would reply. "Isn't that enough?"

And the Beast would give his whistling sigh and vanish.

One day, Beauty looked in her magic mirror and saw her father. He was alone, and he was weeping because he thought she was dead. That night, she asked the Beast if she could visit him. "I'll die of grief if I don't go," she told him.

The Beast said, "I love you too much to refuse you anything. But I know you'll stay with your father once you get there, and then *I'll* be the one who dies of grief."

But Beauty promised faithfully to be back in a week's time, and the Beast said he trusted her to keep her word. "Place your ring on the table next to your bed tonight," he growled, "and you'll wake up at home."

With that, a thousand fireworks exploded over the gardens and there, standing beside Beauty, was a handsome prince – with a rather wet face.

"Where's my Beast?" she asked him.

"I'm him," said the prince. "An enchanter put a spell on me. It made me ugly and stupid. You broke the spell when you said you'd be my wife."

Beauty stared at him in amazement and the prince looked worried.

"I hope you still want to marry me, Beauty, now that I'm not a Beast."

Beauty smiled at him. "I'll get used to you. There's no one in the wide world for me but you, Prince Beast."

"You forgot your promise," he said in a weak voice. "So I starved myself to death. Now I've seen you once more, I shall die in peace." And his eyes closed.

"But you mustn't die," cried Beauty, throwing her arms round him. "Not when I love you so much. Please don't die, my darling Beast. I will marry you. I will be your wife."

Then one night Beauty dreamt she saw the Beast lying in his garden by the fountain. He was dying. She woke in a panic. As she lay in the dark, she remembered the Beast saying that he would die of grief without her. She wondered how she could treat him so cruelly when he had been nothing but kind to her. She put her ring on the table next to her as she had done before. In the morning, she woke up in the Beast's mansion.

Beauty could hardly wait till suppertime to see him. At last the clock struck nine but there was no ear-crunching noise and no Beast. Where was he?

She hurried about the mansion searching for him. Then she remembered her dream. He'd been lying in the garden. She ran across the lawns to the fountain, and there lay the Beast, as still as death. She threw a cupped handful of water over him and he opened his eyes.

The sisters stomped down the garden to plot and plan.

"We'll make her break her promise to return in a week. Then the Beast will eat her," said one.

"We'll beg her to stay when the week is up. We'll pretend we love her to bits," said the other.

"That will be the hardest part," her sister replied.

At the end of the week, that's exactly what they did. They tore their hair and wailed. Tears ran down their cheeks. And Beauty was so happy to see that at long last her sisters really and truly liked her, she didn't mention how strongly they smelt of onion, and agreed to stay on.

"I'm sure the Beast won't mind just one more week," she said. But at the end of that week the same thing happened, and at the end of the following week too.

They began trying the things on but – boom! – in a split second the pretty clothes turned into silly knickers and the sisters had to cover themselves up in Beauty's sheets. The sisters were furious that they had been made to look ridiculous in front of their new husbands, even though the husbands were as boring as washing-up water. One was too clever by half and the other too handsome to be true.

So she did. And when she woke the next morning, she was in her old bed, which was a bit lumpy, she noticed, compared with her bed at the mansion.

Then a servant came running, her sisters came running, their new husbands came running and her father came running. He was so pleased to see her, he could not stop hugging her.

"And look at all these gorgeous clothes she's brought with her," the sisters marvelled, unpacking a trunk that had arrived with Beauty.